My Cat

Written by Monica Hughes

Illustrated by Yvonne Muller

My cat is licking her paw.
Lick, lick, lick.

3

My cat is licking her leg.

Lick, lick, lick.

5

My cat is licking her back.
Lick, lick, lick.

My cat is licking her tail.
Lick, lick, lick.

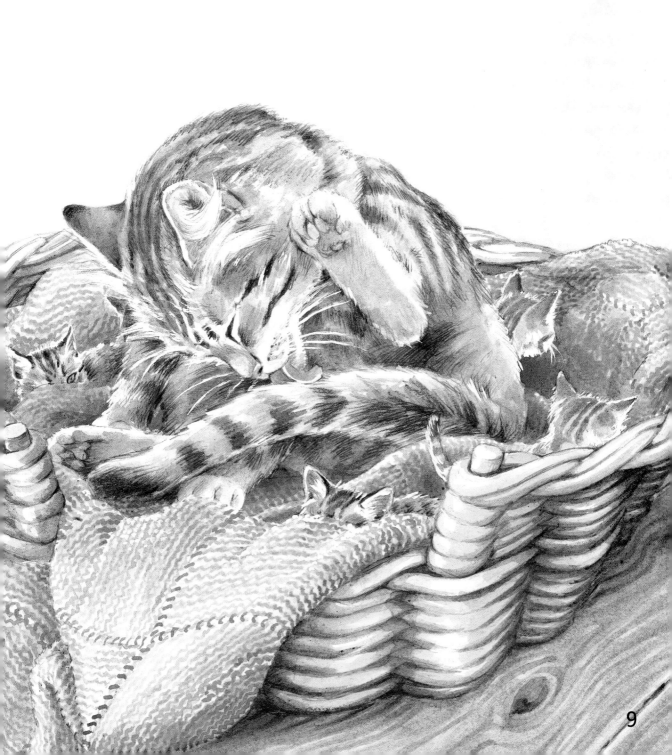

9

My cat is licking her kittens.

Lick, lick, lick, lick, lick.